Desert Life

Carmel Reilly

Contents

Desert Life

Deserts as Homes

Deserts are places that have low rainfall, extreme temperatures and rocky or sandy soils.

There are four main types of deserts:

- **arid** deserts, which are hot and dry
- semi-arid deserts, which have higher rainfall than arid deserts
- coastal deserts, which are near the sea
- polar deserts, which are usually covered in snow and ice.

Deserts cover about 30 per cent of Earth's land.

an arid desert

Although desert environments are usually dry and bare, they are home to many types of living things. These include plants, **fungi**, animals, insects and **microscopic** life such as **bacteria**. Over thousands of years, these have been able to adapt, or change, to survive the harsh desert conditions.

Living things are also able to survive by forming **ecosystems**, where they work together to provide food and shelter for each other within the desert landscape.

Rainfall is measured in millimetres. It tells the average depth of the rainwater that fell on every part of the ground.

Coastal deserts, such as the Atacama Desert in Chile, are found where the land meets the ocean.

Life in Arid Deserts

Arid deserts are found in Africa, Australia, Central Asia and North and South America. Arid deserts are harsh environments where less than 250 millimetres of rain falls each year. In contrast, non-desert environments receive 600–1100 millimetres of rainfall a year.

At Home in the Sahara Desert, North Africa

The Sahara Desert is the largest arid desert in the world. It covers almost a third of the African continent. Despite its extreme conditions, the Sahara is home to hundreds of **species** of plants and animals that have adapted to the dryness and heat.

Date Palm

The date palm is a type of tree that grows well in this hot environment. Date palms have long roots, which allow them to suck moisture from deep in the ground. Their tall, thin trunks allow for air to move around them and keep them cool. The curved branches and thick leaves of date palms also give shade to their trunks and stop them from being burnt by the sun.

date palms in the desert in Tunisia

Sahara Desert Key Facts

Area: approximately 9 000 000 square kilometres

Average temperatures: 36 degrees **Celsius** in summer; 13 degrees Celsius in winter

Average rainfall: 76 millimetres per year

North African Ostrich

The North African ostrich can live for weeks in the Sahara Desert without water. Most of the moisture it needs to survive comes from the food it eats. It has a long, bare neck and long legs, and can raise its feathers away from its body. These features allow air to flow around its body and help to keep it cool. When it is windy in the desert, the ostrich's three eyelids and thick, feathery eyelashes protect its eyes from the desert sands.

A North African ostrich paces through the desert.

Fennec Fox

Fennec foxes avoid the daytime heat in the desert. During the day, they sleep in burrows that they dig in the sand, and they go hunting for food only in the evening when it is cooler. They do not need to drink a lot and can get most of the water they need from their diet of small animals and plants. Fennec foxes have fur on the pads of their feet, which helps to protect them from the scorching desert sand.

Fennec foxes hunt in the cool of the evening.

At Home in the Gibson Desert, Australia

The Gibson Desert is one of a group of deserts in the centre of the Australian continent. It is known for its red sand soils, low and scrubby plants, and blazing hot summer temperatures.

Desert Bloodwood

The desert bloodwood is one of the few trees that grow in the Gibson Desert. It has thick, rough bark that protects it from the sun's heat and from the grass fires that sometimes sweep through the desert. When the heat becomes extreme, this tree drops some of its branches. Having fewer branches makes the tree smaller and reduces its need for water and energy, helping it to survive.

a desert bloodwood

Red Honey Ant

Red honey ants do not have to drink any water. They get all the moisture they need from their diet of dead insects, seeds and scraps of plants. Red honey ants turn the moisture they collect into a type of honey, which they store in their abdomens. They can use it later for energy when their food supplies are low.

Gibson Desert Key Facts

Area: 155 000 square kilometres

Average temperatures: maximum 40 degrees Celsius in summer; 6 degrees Celsius in winter

Average rainfall: 200–250 millimetres per year

Thorny Devil

The Gibson Desert is the perfect home for thorny devils. These cold-blooded creatures need the heat of the sun to keep them warm. This means that they can stay outside during the day when many other creatures need to rest in the shade. Their diet of termites and desert ants provides them with most of their moisture. They can obtain extra water from the **dew** that collects in the grooves on their skin overnight.

Thorny devils are covered in sharp spines.

Red Kangaroo

Red kangaroos can survive the dry desert conditions because most of the water they need comes from the food they eat. They avoid the heat of the sun by being most active during the evenings, when the temperatures are lower. Red kangaroos can cool themselves by panting and by licking their chest and arm fur to make it wet.

Red kangaroos can travel at more than 50 kilometres per hour. They can leap almost 8 metres in one jump.

red kangaroos

Life in Semi-Arid Deserts

Semi-arid deserts are found on many continents. These deserts receive higher rainfall than arid deserts and their temperatures are usually lower. There are two types of semi-arid deserts: cold and hot. Cold semi-arid deserts have hot summers and very cold winters. Hot semi-arid deserts usually have hot summers and mild winters.

At Home in the Great Basin Desert, USA

The Great Basin Desert is a cold semi-arid desert with long and often snowy winters. It covers a vast area of the western part of the USA that includes mountains, valleys and plains. This desert is home to many types of living things.

Great Basin Desert Key Facts

Area: 492 000 square kilometres

Average temperatures: maximum 30 degrees Celsius in summer; 5 degrees Celsius in winter

Average rainfall: 350 millimetres per year

Great Basin Sagebrush

The Great Basin sagebrush is a small, hardy bush. It can survive with little water and in places that are very cold in winter. This plant has a root system that is both wide and deep. The wide roots help it to soak up rainwater that collects near the top of the ground. The deep roots allow it to reach moisture that is stored deeper in the soil.

Great Basin sagebrush grows well in dry, rocky soils.

Sagebrush Vole

Sagebrush voles are small animals that live among sagebrush. They feed on grasses and seeds in summer, and on sagebrush in winter. These foods provide them with most of their water needs. Sagebrush voles make their homes in burrows that they dig under the roots of the sagebrush. Their grey fur blends in with the soil and brush roots. This helps them to hide from predators.

a sagebrush vole

Darkling Beetle

Darkling beetles thrive in semi-arid desert conditions. This is because they need little water and can avoid the summer sun by being active at night. Darkling beetles are **decomposers** and will eat whatever they find around them, including rotting plants and animals, dead insects and fungi. They break these materials down in their bodies into **fertiliser**, which feeds desert plant life.

a darkling beetle

Mountain Lion

The mountain lions of the Great Basin Desert live in caves and holes in rocks, where they spend the days avoiding the sun. In the evenings, they roam across large areas of desert in search of prey. As food is often scarce, they will eat whatever they can hunt. Like many desert animals, they have adapted to their environment and can exist for long periods without drinking water.

Mountain lions avoid the sun by sheltering in caves and holes in rocks.

At Home in the Thar Desert, India and Pakistan

The Thar Desert receives up to 500 millimetres of rain each year, which makes it wetter than most deserts. Almost all this rain falls between June and September. Throughout the rest of the year, heat and strong winds dry out the soil.

Raptors

Many raptors, or hunting birds, live in the Thar Desert. They include eagles, falcons, kestrels and vultures. They eat small animals, reptiles and other birds, which also provide most of their water.

A falcon flies low over the desert in search of prey.

Thar Desert Key Facts

Area: 200 000 square kilometres

Average temperatures: maximum 48 degrees Celsius in summer; 10 degrees Celsius in winter

Average rainfall: 300 millimetres per year

Chestnut-bellied Sandgrouse

Most birds in the Thar Desert get enough water from their food. However, some birds, such as the chestnut-bellied sandgrouse, need to drink fresh water. The sandgrouse flies up to 80 kilometres every day to find water. The male sandgrouse can carry some of this water back to his chicks. He does this by soaking up small amounts of liquid into his stomach feathers, which he releases when he returns to the nest.

A chestnut-bellied sandgrouse drinks water early in the day.

Common Krait

The common krait is one of 25 species of snakes that live in the Thar Desert. While it needs the heat of the day to warm its blood, this snake does not like extremely high temperatures. It avoids the hottest part of the day by resting in a cool, dark place. At night, when the temperature is cooler, the krait becomes very active and hunts small animals, insects and reptiles, including other snakes.

A common krait rests in a cool place during the day.

Indian Grey Mongoose

The Indian grey mongoose is a small, furry mammal that is common in the Thar Desert. It avoids the desert heat by sleeping during the day in a burrow in the sandy soil. It is especially active at dawn and dusk, when it hunts its prey. The mongoose's diet includes small animals, reptiles, birds and insects. It often hunts and eats snakes as it is **immune** to the poison in snake bites.

An Indian grey mongoose attacks a snake.

Life in Coastal Deserts

Coastal deserts are found next to oceans. They are both drier and cooler than other types of deserts. Most coastal deserts are on the western shores of North and South America, and Africa.

At Home in the Atacama Desert, Chile

The Atacama Desert is a narrow strip of desert that stretches more than 1000 kilometres along the west coast of South America. It is bordered by the Pacific Ocean to the west and the Andes (pronounced *an-deez*) Mountains to the east. It is one of the driest places in the world. In some years it has no rainfall. However, the Atacama Desert does receive a small amount of moisture from morning fog that rolls in from the sea.

Atacama Desert Key Facts

Area: 105 000 square kilometres

Average temperatures: maximum 24 degrees Celsius in summer; 20 degrees Celsius in winter

Average rainfall: 15 millimetres per year

Tillandsia

Tillandsias (pronounced *tah-land-zee-ahs*) are plants that survive well in the Atacama Desert. They grow on loose desert soil, rocks or other plants. Tillandsias do not have a root system and cannot take water from the ground. They get all the water they need from fog that rolls in from the sea. Their scaly leaves capture this moisture, and also protect them from the heat of the sun.

Tillandsias grow in the loose soil of the Atacama Desert.

Darwin's Leaf-Eared Mouse

Darwin's leaf-eared mouse is one of the few mammals that live in the Atacama Desert. This mouse survives by eating whatever food it can find, including insects, seeds and grasses. This diet provides almost all the water it needs. Its sand-coloured fur allows it to blend in with the desert and dry grasses around it. This helps to keep it safe from predators, which include reptiles, desert foxes, eagles and hawks.

A Darwin's leaf-eared mouse blends in with its desert habitat.

Bacteria

It was once believed that nothing could live in the very driest part of the Atacama Desert. However, in recent years, scientists have discovered at least 30 species of bacteria there. Bacteria are tiny life forms that can be seen only with a microscope. The bacteria live in slightly damp soil, about 30 centimetres below the surface. They get just enough moisture and minerals from the soil around them to survive.

Bacteria have been found in the soil of the Atacama Desert.

Life in Polar Deserts

Polar deserts are located in the Arctic and Antarctic. They have low rainfall, low summer temperatures and extremely low temperatures in winter. Like all deserts, they have rocky or sandy soil. However, this soil is covered in ice and snow for most of the year.

At Home in the Arctic Polar Desert

The Arctic is the northern-most region of Earth. It is the world's second-largest desert after Antarctica. The central part of the Arctic is frozen all year round. The outer areas are mostly made up of **tundra**, where there is snow only in the winter.

This map shows the Arctic Polar Desert in winter, when there is more ice.

Reindeer Cup Lichen

Reindeer cup **lichen** is made up of bacteria and fungi. It is abundant in the Arctic, where it grows on the surface of rocks, even with low levels of light and water.

Reindeer cup lichen gets most of the water it needs from rain, but it can also obtain moisture from dust in the air. It finds the minerals it needs by breaking down the rocks where it grows. When there is no rain, reindeer cup lichen dries out and becomes **dormant**. When the rain returns, it can quickly soak up the moisture and return to how it was.

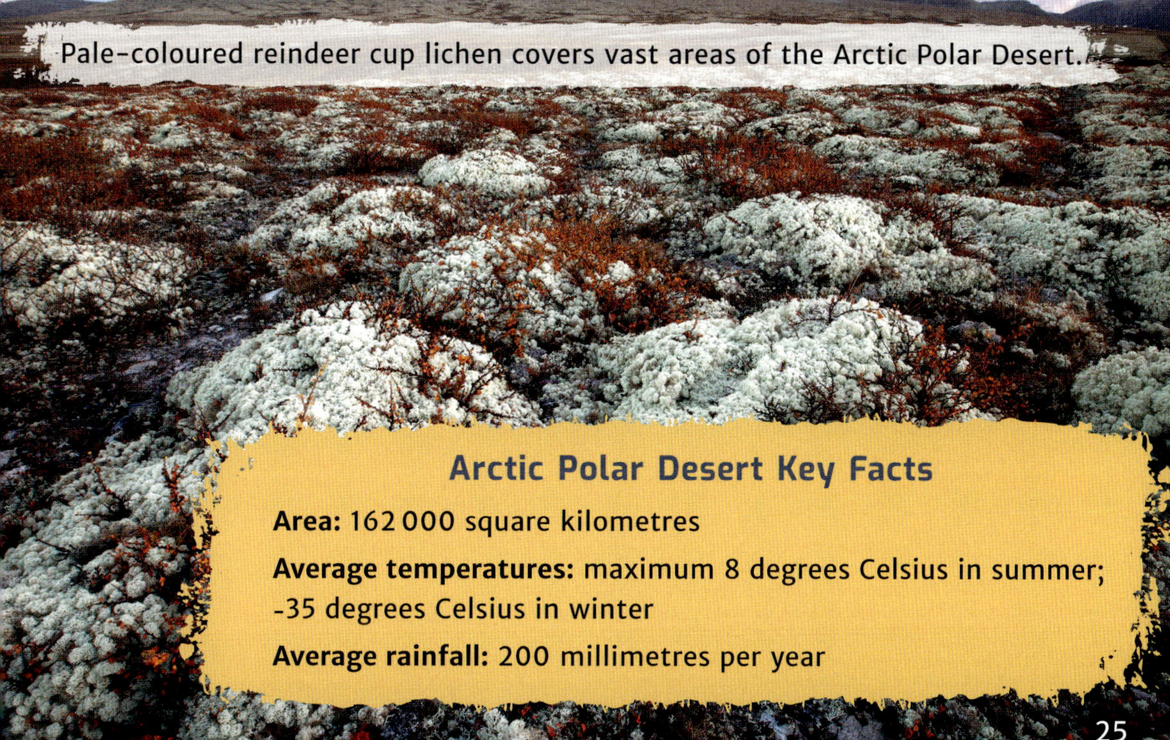

Pale-coloured reindeer cup lichen covers vast areas of the Arctic Polar Desert.

Arctic Polar Desert Key Facts

Area: 162 000 square kilometres

Average temperatures: maximum 8 degrees Celsius in summer; -35 degrees Celsius in winter

Average rainfall: 200 millimetres per year

Arctic Fox

Artic foxes have very thick fur, which keeps them warm during winter in the Arctic Polar Desert. Their fur changes colour from white in winter to brown in summer. This colour change helps them blend in with their surroundings so they are not seen by predators, such as polar bears.

Arctic foxes live in burrows where they can keep warm in winter. They eat almost anything they can find, from mice to seaweed. In summer, Arctic foxes eat extra food to build up layers of fat under their skin. Their bodies use up this extra fat during the winter when there is less food available.

The Arctic fox has thick, white fur in winter.

Reindeer

Reindeer have two layers of fur to help keep them warm in winter. The outer layer **moults** in spring, leaving the reindeer cooler in the summer months. They have large feet with two toes and two claws. These features help them to walk over snow in winter and to dig for food in the tundra in summer. In winter, their diet is made up almost entirely of lichen. Reindeer are hunted by wolves, eagles and bears.

Reindeer's fur helps keep them warm in winter.

How a Desert Ecosystem Works

An ecosystem is a community of living things that work together to create a network of life within a landscape and climate. In a desert ecosystem, this community exists in very dry and **sparse** environments with extreme (hot or cold) temperatures.

Living things in an ecosystem play four key roles: producers, consumers, predators and decomposers. In some desert landscapes, living things may have more than one role.

Producers

Plants are the desert's producers. They can range from tiny grasses to large trees. They provide food and shelter for many other desert life forms.

Consumers

Living things that rely on producers for food and shelter are called consumers. These can range from fungi, insects and birds to small and large animals. In turn, consumers become food for predators.

Predators

Predators prey on both consumers and other predators. They do not eat more than they need and tend to eat sick or weaker creatures. This helps to keep the consumer and predator populations healthy.

Decomposers

Bacteria, insects and fungi are decomposers. They help break down animal and plant waste. This creates fertiliser, which is used to feed plants and help them grow. Decomposers often become food for consumers.

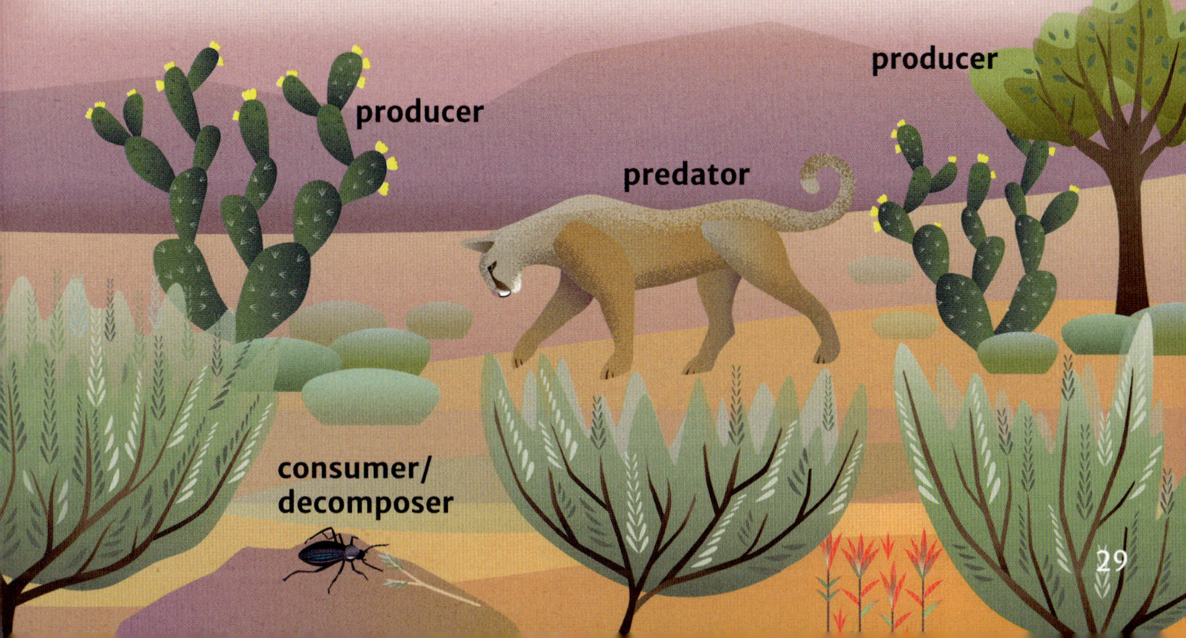

Living Deserts

There are many different desert environments around the world. Desert climates range from the sizzling heat of arid deserts to the harsh cold of polar deserts.

Living things have adapted to survive in all of these environments, despite extreme temperatures and little water.

Glossary

arid (*adjective*) very hot and dry

bacteria (*noun*) tiny living things found in all natural environments

Celsius (*adjective*) on a scale for measuring temperature

decomposers (*noun*) organisms that cause something to decay

dew (*noun*) tiny drops of water that form at night

dormant (*adjective*) alive but not active

ecosystems (*noun*) communities of plants and animals living together in an environment

fertiliser (*noun*) a substance that helps plants to grow

fungi (*noun*) plant-like living things, such as moulds or mushrooms

immune (*adjective*) having natural protection against disease or poison

lichen (*noun*) a slow-growing, crusty plant that grows on rocks and trees

microscopic (*adjective*) so small it can only be seen with a microscope

moults (*verb*) sheds old feathers, fur or skin to make way for new growth

sparse (*adjective*) spread out over a wide area

species (*noun*) particular types of animals

tundra (*noun*) a very cold area with hard, frozen ground where trees do not grow

Index